The
Hairy Flip-Flops
And Other Fulani Folk Tales

Written by
Stephen Davies

Illustrated by
Steve Stone

The Hairy Flip-Flops

Hyena lived in Mali, on the edge of the great Sahara Desert. He had four cubs, which he kept in a tiny burrow, protected from the blistering heat of day and the biting cold of night.

One day, the same as always, Hyena went to the burrow with a hunk of meat for his cubs. But instead of throwing in the meat as he usually did, he decided to summon his cubs outside. "I haven't seen you in weeks," he called. "Come out and show your father how big and strong you've grown!"

One by one, the cubs wriggled out of the burrow, but they were neither big nor strong. Far from it. They were the skinniest cubs Hyena had ever seen.

"Look at yourselves!" Hyena cried. "Bony backs, lanky legs, flaky fur. What's wrong with you? Every day I work my tail off to bring you good food, but you lot look as if you haven't eaten for weeks!"

"We haven't," piped up the smallest cub. "Someone is stealing our meat, Papa, and selling it at the market. He's in there right now, Papa, just waiting for you to throw the meat in."

4

"What?!" The hackles rose on Hyena's back. "What does he look like, this meat thief?"

"He's got long ears and buck teeth and a fluffy tail and —"

"Rabbit!" Hyena yelled. "Is that you in there?"

There was a short silence and then a cheerful voice came from the burrow. "Hello Hyena, old friend," called the voice. "You've caught me good and proper this time."

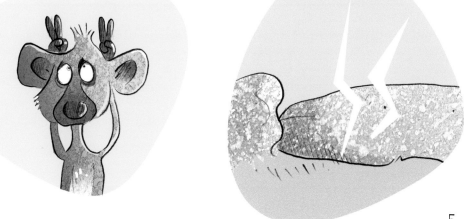

"Come out, this minute!" yelled Hyena, who was too big to go into the burrow himself.

"I'm not surprised you're angry," said Rabbit. "After all, this isn't the first time I've tricked you, is it? Do you remember when I gave you that dead hen in exchange for ten live ones?"

Hyena winced at the memory. "You told me that hen was asleep," he snarled. "You said it was a very special hen and it would lay a golden egg as soon as it woke up."

A peal of laughter came from the dark burrow. "Remember when
I bet you that you couldn't eat a banana in a minute?"

Hyena scowled. "You never told me Scorpion was hiding underneath
that banana!"

"What about the time you fell asleep under the neem tree and I
painted your tail blue? How we all laughed that day!"

7

Hyena stood up on his hind legs
and raked the air furiously with his
sharp claws. "Come out this minute!"
he roared. "Then we'll see who
has the last laugh!"

"All right, I'm coming out,"
said Rabbit, who did not
sound scared at all. "But listen,
old friend, I'm worried that
the hot sand will burn my
paws. Here's what I'll do.
I'll pass you my flip-flops
and you can lay them down
for me just outside the burrow
for me to step into.
There's a good fellow."

A pair of flip-flops poked up out of the burrow, but Hyena hardly looked at them. Rabbit's list of tricks had succeeded in working Hyena up into a blind rage, and the only thing in the world he cared about was getting his paws on his old enemy.

"Come out and face me!" cried Hyena, grabbing the flip-flops and throwing them away from him as hard and far as he could.

Even through the red mist of his anger, Hyena couldn't help noticing that the flip-flops were heavier and hairier than normal flip-flops. In fact, as they unfolded in midair they no longer looked like flip-flops at all. They looked like – oh, no! – like long, hairy ears attached to a chuckling rabbit!

Rabbit landed on his feet at a safe distance. "Thanks for helping me escape, Hyena," he yelled. "And thanks for all the meat – I've been getting a very good price for it!"

Hyena gnashed his teeth and pounced at Rabbit, but the little creature had a good head start and dashed hippety-hop away into the desert as fast as the Harmattan wind. Hyena chased him a short distance, then stopped, exhausted.

Rabbit turned and peformed a little victory dance. "We rabbits don't need to wear flip-flops, old friend!" he shouted. "We're fast enough without them!"

Bravery Is for Wimps

One hot day on the edge of the great Sahara, Hyena and Jackal were chatting in the shade of a baobab tree, and their talk turned to the subject of bravery. A crowd of other animals gathered to listen in on their boastful conversation.

"Bravery's in my blood," Jackal said. "I'm the bravest creature in the bush."

"Ha!" scoffed Hyena. "Bravery's for wimps."

Jackal scowled. His hackles rose. "What do you mean by that?"

"Being brave means overcoming fear," said Hyena. "But me, I feel no fear in the first place. In fact, brother Jackal, I can't think of a single thing I'm afraid of."

All the animals gasped in admiration.

Jackal's eyes narrowed. "You're not afraid of bees?"

"No."

"Scorpions?"

"Not at all."

"What about –" Jackal lowered his voice, "man?"

Hyena shook his head haughtily. "Not in the slightest."

"I bet you couldn't ride a lion!" said a voice in Hyena's ear.

Hyena spun round and saw a little creature hiding in the hollow of the baobab tree, a cheeky little creature with long ears and buck teeth. Rabbit! Not again!

Hyena's first instinct was to pounce on his enemy and take him home for the pot, but he could feel everybody's eyes on him. They expected him to reply to Rabbit's challenge.

"What a foolish idea, Brother Rabbit," blustered Hyena.
"No animal would ride a lion."

"I would," said Rabbit, hopping out of his hollow.

"Ride away," Hyena laughed, "you'll be lucky to last five seconds."

"I've got an idea," said Rabbit, twirling his ears, "let's all go to Lion's
den next Friday morning, and you can see for yourselves who's
the most fearless animal in the land."

The animals agreed and went home chattering among themselves about Rabbit's fearlessness.

Hyena clenched his paws as he watched them go. How dare Rabbit show him up in public! Never mind, he thought. Next Friday I can enjoy watching that pesky rabbit being eaten by Lion.

Rabbit didn't go straight home. Instead he went to the butcher's stall at the market. While the butcher was looking the other way, Rabbit hopped up on to the stall, grabbed a hunk of meat and hurried off with it.

Rabbit scampered unobserved to Lion's den, stopping 20 metres away. As soon as Lion emerged into the light, Rabbit threw down the meat, bowed respectfully and ran off home.

17

The following morning Rabbit returned to the butcher's stall and stole a second hunk of meat. He took it to Lion's den and laid it down 10 metres from the entrance. He bowed low and ran off home.

Every day Rabbit went back to Lion's den with hunks of meat, and every day he ventured closer and closer to the mouth of the den. By Thursday he was able to go right up to Lion and stroke his glossy fur while he ate his meat. His plan was coming together nicely.

Friday morning dawned clear and bright. The animals gathered in an anxious semicircle around Lion's den. Hyena and Jackal were there, of course, chuckling and nudging one another.

Along came Rabbit, grinning cheekily. He hopped right up to the mouth of the den and cried, "Salaam alaikum, Lion!"

Lion loped into the sunlight. He frowned when he saw the crowd
of animals.

"Forgive me, Your Highness," Rabbit whispered in his ear, "the butcher
has no meat today. But if you'd grant me the honour of sitting on
your powerful back for a few moments, I'll bring you
an extra big piece tomorrow."

"Just make sure you do," snarled Lion. It was all very well this rabbit turning up and bringing him meat, but his patience would only stretch so far.

Rabbit hopped on to Lion's back and sat there grinning as he paced back and forth in front of his den. The other animals looked on in wide-eyed astonishment, and poor Hyena was so stunned, he fainted.

By the time Hyena came round, all the spectators had left.
To Hyena's horror, Lion was standing over him, licking his lips.

"Thank you for sticking around," Lion growled, "I was wondering
where I'd find my breakfast this morning."

22

Hyena sprang to his feet and dashed away into the bush, pursued by Lion. As they passed the hollow baobab tree, a rabbity voice piped up loud and clear.

"Run as fast as you can, old friend! Bravery is for wimps!"

Animals Do What Animals Do

On a hot Saharan morning, a boy called Hamma was herding his father's goats. He used a staff to shake down seed pods from the thorn trees and the goats rushed to and fro, munching and crunching and bleating happily.

As soon as the goats had eaten their fill, Hamma led them down to the watering hole. But when he arrived, his heart sank. The earth was parched and cracked, and the water in the hole had shrunk to a small, muddy puddle, nowhere near enough water for thirty thirsty goats. They'd have to go all the way to the Great River instead.

As Hamma turned to leave, he heard a pathetic, rasping cry. The cry sounded like "Help," but where was it coming from?

Hamma looked around. A pair of hooded eyes gazed pleadingly at him from the far side of the muddy puddle. The eyes blinked, and out of the hole heaved a long, mud-caked face. Hamma's goats backed away, bleating in fright.

"Crocodile!" gasped Hamma.

"Help me," repeated Crocodile, "if you don't, I'll die here."

Never go near Crocodile, Hamma's parents always told him. He can't be trusted.

But this was different. Crocodile was stranded in this dried-up watering hole. What harm could he do? Hamma kicked off his shoes and tiptoed across the dry, cracked earth towards the mud where Crocodile lay. He spread his arms round Crocodile's large, mud-caked body and heaved with all his might.

"Good boy," said Crocodile, "that's the way."

"It's impossible to pick you up," panted Hamma. "You're such an awkward shape."

Nearby stood an old nomad hut made of long grass mats stretched over a frame of sticks. Hamma had an idea. He went to the hut, untied the longest grass mat and dragged it across to where Crocodile lay. He laid it down on top of the mud and rolled Crocodile on to one edge. Then he rolled up Crocodile inside the mat and hoisted the whole package on to his shoulders.

"Good boy," said Crocodile, "that's the way."

Puffing and panting, Hamma carried Crocodile all the way to the Great River, followed by thirty surprised goats. When they arrived, Hamma waded into the shallows and dropped Crocodile in. But as soon as Crocodile hit the water, Crocodile twisted his tail round Hamma's waist and started to drag him off into deeper water.

"That's wrong," spluttered Hamma, struggling to get away from the deceitful beast. "You can't eat me! I just saved your life!"

"It's not wrong at all," said Crocodile. "Showing kindness is what humans do best, and eating humans is what crocodiles do best. Animals do what animals do, my friend. There's nothing wrong with that!"

Just then, along came Rabbit, hopping along the river bank towards them. Fresh from tricking Hyena, he was grinning all over his whiskery face.

"Very well," said Hamma, "let's ask Rabbit to judge our case. He's the smartest animal I know. He can tell us whether you're wrong to eat someone who just saved your life."

"Why not?" said Crocodile smoothly. He was quite certain that Rabbit would be on his side and that he'd soon be eating Hamma for lunch.

Crocodile kept his tail firmly around Hamma's waist as they took turns to tell Rabbit their story. Rabbit listened carefully.

"It's impossible to judge," said Rabbit at last, "unless I can picture exactly what happened. Show me, Crocodile, how Hamma carried you."

"Like this!" said Crocodile. He let go of Hamma, dragged himself up on to the bank and allowed himself to be rolled up in the mat once more.

"I see," said Rabbit, "but it's still impossible to judge unless I can picture exactly what happened. Show me, Hamma, where you first met Crocodile."

"Come!" said Hamma, and he carried Crocodile all the way back to the dried-up watering hole.

"I see," said Rabbit, "but it's impossible to judge unless I can picture exactly what happened. Show me, Crocodile, where you were lying."

"Right here!" said Crocodile. He slid out of the grass mat and plopped down into the thick mud on the far side of the watering hole.

33

"Very good," said Rabbit. "I have reached my decision, and I am deciding in favour of Crocodile. Animals do what animals do, my friends. You, Hamma, were right to save Crocodile, and you, Crocodile, were right to try and eat him."

"Told you!" said Crocodile, but when he saw Hamma and Rabbit turning to leave, his triumphant grin turned to a frown. "Hey, where are you going? You have to take me back to the river now. Hey, come back!"

"So long, Crocodile!" called Rabbit. "Hamma was right to save you, you were right to try and eat him, and I was right to trick you. Animals do what animals do, my friend. There's nothing wrong with that."

Off Rabbit hopped, shaking with laughter. He had managed to outwit another foolish creature. And with any luck, there would be time for one more trick before the day was out.

Dead Donkeys

As the sun dipped low over the great
Sahara, Hyena left his den and loped
among the thorny trees in search of
an evening meal. Fresh meat or rotten,
Hyena didn't mind. Satisfying his hunger
pangs was all he cared about.

Around the back of a hollow baobab tree, Hyena found a dead donkey. It couldn't have died more than two days before because it was only a little bit smelly. What a stroke of luck!

Hyena grinned from ear to ear and bent his head to feast. But before he had a chance to start his meal, he was interrupted by the sound of scampering paws nearby.

Peering around the baobab tree, Hyena saw his four cubs lolloping towards him. They must have followed his tracks all the way from the den. How annoying! His cubs should have been big and bad enough by now to hunt and scavenge for themselves. But no, they insisted on following him instead. How dared they spoil his dinner by turning up uninvited!

Hyena thought fast. If the cubs came any further and saw the dead donkey, he'd have no choice but to share it with them. They'd wolf it down like the greedy scavengers they were, and he'd end up with hardly any for himself. No, they mustn't be allowed to see the donkey.

"Cubs, what a joy to see you!" he cried, jumping out from behind the baobab tree. "You're in luck. I just saw your uncle, and he told me that there's a whole herd of dead donkeys lying among the dunes just north of here. Be off with you, my bouncing babes. Go and feast to your hearts' content."

The cubs laughed greedily and their eyes bulged with excitement. Off they dashed towards the north, clouds of red-brown dust billowing from their heels. As soon as they were out of sight, Hyena slipped back round to the other side of the tree and began to eat his dinner, feeling very pleased with himself indeed.

39

A mile or two south of Hyena, hovering high in the sky, a bald old bird with beady eyes surveyed the terrain ahead. Vulture (for it was he) could not help noticing a pack of hyena cubs to the north, and they were racing towards the desert. Vulture knew everything there was to know about hyenas, and he knew what it means when a hyena moves faster than a shuffle. It means meat.

Vulture had no intention of letting a mob of dirty hyenas beat him to a source of good meat. He set off northwards, beating the air with his powerful wings.

Down on the ground a column of soldier ants were marching along in search of supper. Glancing up, their leader noticed that Vulture was no longer circling aimlessly, but flying straight and strong.

"Meat!" cried Ant. "Quick march!"

41

Lying in the fork of a cypress tree, Wild Cat saw the soldier ants swing northwards on the double. Guessing that something meaty was afoot, she stretched, leapt down and shot off north.

Jackal was dozing peacefully when a blur of teeth and claws flew past. He yawned, blinked twice, and joined the race. If Wild Cat was moving that fast, there must be something worth eating and he wasn't going to miss out on a feast.

Meanwhile, behind the baobab tree, Hyena had hardly started his dinner when he became aware of a great commotion. All around him were sprinting jackals, scrambling wild cats and sky-rocketing vultures. It seemed to Hyena as if every meat-lover in the land was dashing north.

"Great!" he thought to himself. "There must be fresh meat up north – and lots of it! I'm not going to waste another moment with this stinking donkey. Full belly, here I come!"

With that, Hyena left his meal and joined the animal dash. Last we heard, he's still running.

The stars came out above the great Sahara Desert.
Inside the hollow of the baobab tree, a long-eared
buck-toothed creature held his sides and laughed
until he cried.

Trick-o-meter

Ideas for reading

Written by Clare Dowdall, PhD
Lecturer and Primary Literacy Consultant

Reading objectives:

- identify themes and conventions
- discuss their understanding
  and explain the meaning
  of words in context
- draw inferences and justify
  these with evidence
- make predictions from details
  stated and applied

Spoken language objectives:

- use spoken language to
  develop understanding through
  speculating, hypothesizing,
  imagining and exploring ideas
- speak audibly and fluently

Curriculum links: Geography
– locational knowledge

Resources: ICT for research

Build a context for reading

- Look at the front cover and read the title. Ask children to identify the creatures and describe what is happening.

- Read the blurb and discuss the meaning of interesting words: trickery, antics, outwit. Check that children understand these words and how they may relate to the stories inside.

- Ask children to suggest any traditional animal tales that they know, e.g. the hare and the tortoise. Discuss what often happens in these stories.

Understand and apply reading strategies

- Read pp2–3 with the children. Ask children to suggest why the hyena cubs were so skinny and what might have been happening to their food.

- Turn to pp4–5. Ask for volunteers to read aloud in role. Develop children's use of expression and intonation by discussing how each character's voice might sound, and noticing punctuation.

- Ask children to read to the end of the first tale (p11). Discuss the events in the story and establish Rabbit's and Hyena's characters and relationship.